The MIXED-UP TRUCK

BY STEPHEN SAVAGE

A NEAL PORTER BOOK
ROARING BROOK PRESS
NEW YORK

Copyright © 2016 by Stephen Savage
A Neal Porter Book
Published by Roaring Brook Press
Roaring Brook Press is a division of Holtzbrinck Publishing Holdings Limited Partnership
175 Fifth Avenue, New York, New York 10010
The artwork for this book was created using digital techniques.
mackids.com

Library of Congress Control Number: 2015034416

ISBN: 978-1-62672-153-1

Our books may be purchased in bulk for promotional, educational, or business use. Please
contact your local bookseller or the Macmillan Corporate and Premium Sales Department
at (800) 221-7945 ext. 5442 or by e-mail at MacmillanSpecialMarkets@macmillan.com.

First edition 2016
Printed in China by Toppan Leefung Printing Ltd., Dongguan City, Guangdong Province

1   3   5   7   9   10   8   6   4   2

For Kirk

It was the cement mixer's
first day on the job.
All the other trucks
were hard at work.

DANGER

CONSTRUCTION
AREA
KEEP OUT

The crane was lifting.

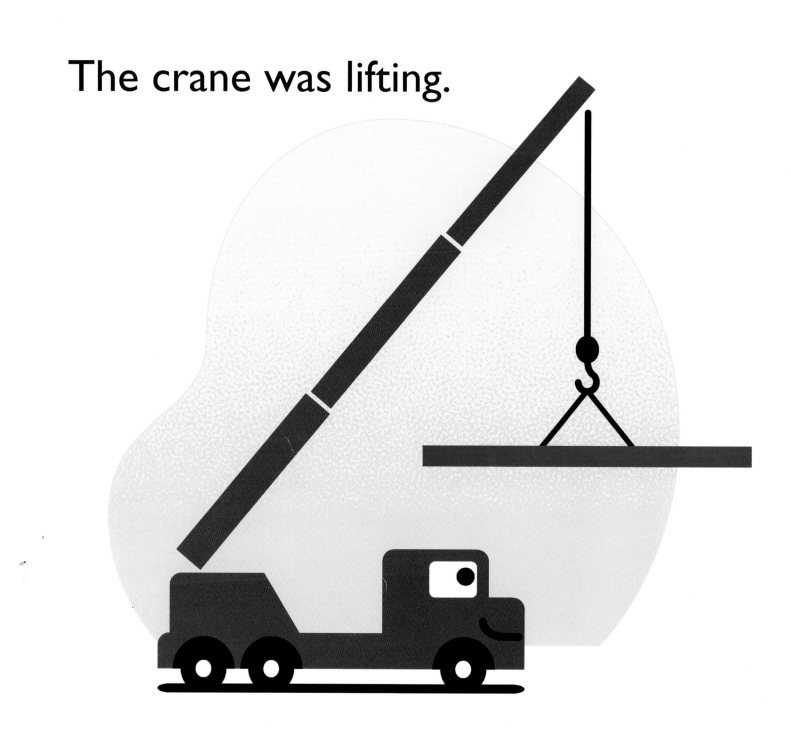

The dump truck
was dumping.

The digger
was digging.

"How can I help?"
asked the cement mixer.
"Mix up some powdery white cement,"
said the trucks.

The cement mixer mixed up
the white powder, added
a little water, and presto!

A CAKE!

"You got mixed up,"
said the trucks.
"Go mix up some powdery
white cement."

The cement mixer mixed up
the white powder, added
a little water, and presto!

FROSTING!

"You got mixed up again," said the trucks. "Go mix up some powdery white cement."

The cement mixer mixed up the white powder, added a little water, and presto!

CEMENT

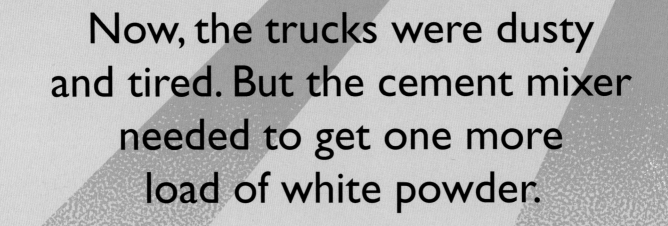

Now, the trucks were dusty
and tired. But the cement mixer
needed to get one more
load of white powder.

The cement mixer mixed up
the white powder, added a
little water, and presto!

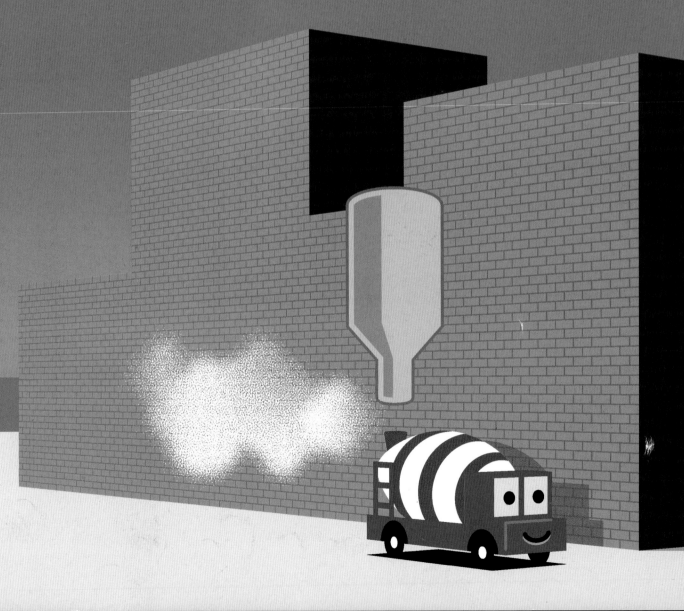

A BUBBLE BATH!